DO YOU WANT TO BE MY FRIEND ?

LC Card Number 70-140643
ISBN 0-690-24276-X
ISBN 0-690-01137-7 (lib. bdg.)
ISBN 0-06-443127-4 (pbk.)

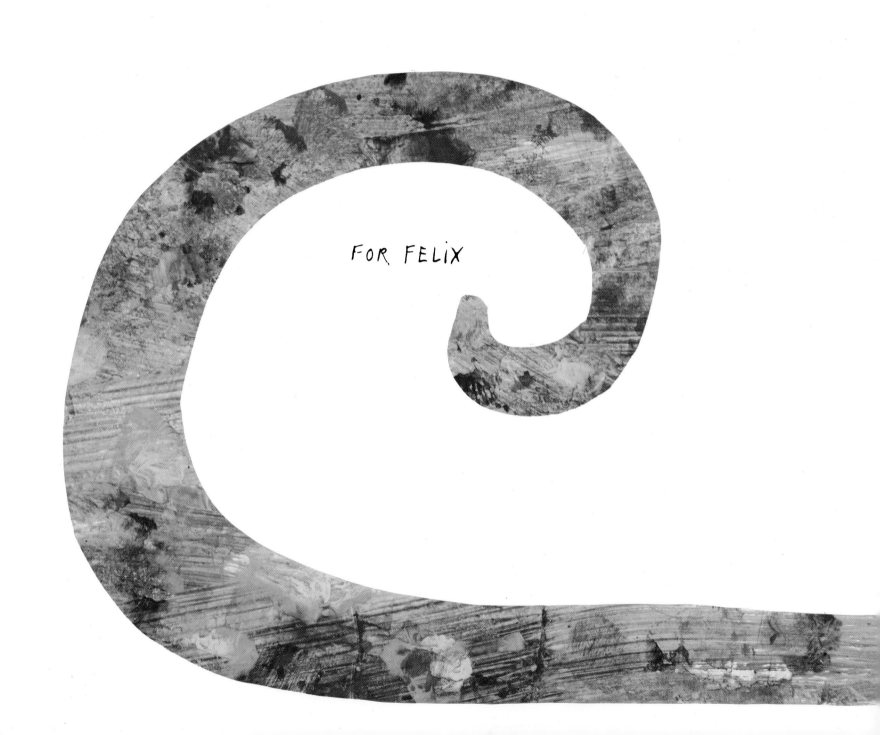

FOR FELIX

A NOTE TO PARENTS AND TEACHERS

This book has been designed to be a very first step toward real reading. There is beauty here, and fun—but there is learning too. Specially planned for the prereading child, this book teaches basic skills of reading readiness. The ingenious placement of the pictures shows the child the correct direction in which to turn the pages. The simple but strong story, even without words, must be "read" from left to right, instilling the idea of linear sequences and forming a groundwork on which to build correct reading habits.

A little help may be needed to start the very young child off, but he will quickly get the idea and will happily improvise his own story, based on Eric Carle's striking pictures. When Mr. Carle tells the story himself, he begins something like this: "Little Mouse was lonely. He wanted a friend to play with. 'Do you want to be my friend?' he asked the horse. But the horse was so busy eating he did not seem to hear Little Mouse at all. 'Never mind,' said Little Mouse to himself. 'I see a long, green tail over there. Perhaps it belongs to someone who will be my friend.' But *that* tail belonged to an alligator, who was not at all friendly. And the next belonged to a lion. And the next…"

Though told almost entirely without words, this book has a definite plot and a subplot, a hero and an antagonist. The latter is in plain view throughout but unsuspected of villainy until the exciting climax, as in all well-constructed suspense stories, and the ending is happy and satisfying. Small children will delight in the surprise and adventure brought by each turn of the page as Little Mouse looks for—and finally finds—a friend. At the same time, they will be acquiring important prereading skills.

DO YOU WANT TO BE MY FRIEND?

BY ERIC CARLE

HarperCollinsPublishers

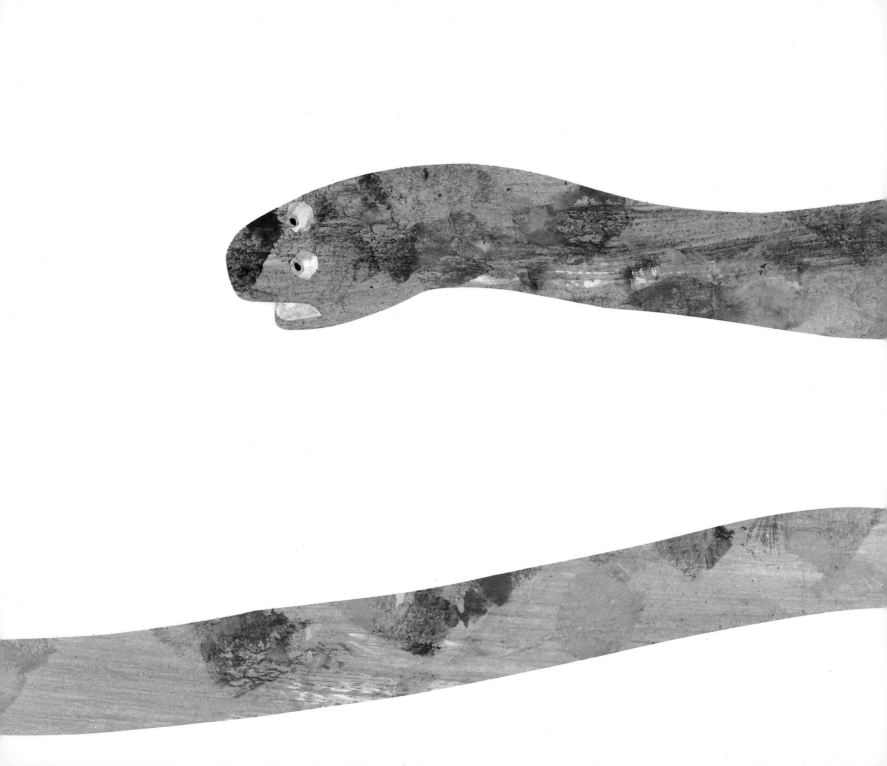